TA058428

Weekly Reader Books presents

NO ONE
NOTICED
RALPH

Doubleday & Company, Inc., Garden City, New York

NO ONE NOTICED RALPH

by Bonnie Bishop
illustrated by Jack Kent

To Debby, Bart, and the Real Ralph

Library of Congress Catalog Card Number 78-18555

ISBN 0-385-12158-X Trade

ISBN 0-385-12159-8 Prebound

Text Copyright © 1979 by Ruth W. Bishop

Illustrations Copyright © 1979 by Jack Kent

Ralph was a parrot.

He lived in the city

with Mr. and Mrs. Muggs.

Mr. Muggs was a teacher.

He taught math

in a school.

Mrs. Muggs was an artist.

She worked in an office

and drew pictures for

birthday cards.

Ralph was happy living

with Mr. and Mrs. Muggs.

He had his own perch to sit on

and his own water dish.

Ralph could whistle

and say several words.

He was proud that he could talk

because it made people notice him.

HELLO!

Every morning Ralph woke up
at seven o'clock.

He would shake himself
all over.

He would take
a drink of water.

Then he would
whistle loudly.

Mr. and Mrs. Muggs would wake up.

"Hello, Ralph!" they would say.

Ralph would answer, "Hello!"

Then Mr. and Mrs. Muggs

would get up.

They would get dressed

and go to work.

On Saturdays Ralph would not

whistle until eleven o'clock.

That was because Mr. and Mrs.

Muggs liked to sleep late.

One Saturday, Ralph forgot

what day it was.

He whistled at seven o'clock.

Mr. and Mrs. Muggs

got up.

They got dressed

and went to work.

When Mrs. Muggs
got to her office,
no one was there.

When Mr. Muggs
got to his school,
it was closed.

They were not happy

when they came home.

"Did you forget that

it is Saturday?"

they asked Ralph.

Ralph felt foolish.

After that, he was more careful

about remembering what day it was.

Ralph loved

to eat crackers.

He liked the kind

with sesame seeds on top.

When he was hungry,

he would say,

"Give me a cracker."

Mr. and Mrs. Muggs
would get him one
from the box.

They could not
leave the box open,
because when it came
to eating crackers,
Ralph did not know when to stop.

When Ralph wanted someone
to notice him,

he would say,

"I love you!"

It always worked.

Mr. Muggs would st[op]
reading his book and
come over to Ralp[h].

Mrs. Muggs would stop drawing pictures
and come over too.

Mr. Muggs liked to tease
and tickle Ralph.

And Ralph liked to
tease and tickle
Mr. Muggs.

Mrs. Muggs liked to scratch
Ralph on the neck.

And Ralph liked
to nibble Mrs. Muggs
on the chin.

Ralph's favorite time was
in the evening.

On cold, winter evenings,

Mr. and Mrs. Muggs would

sit around the fireplace

and eat popcorn.

Ralph would remind them

by saying, "Fire!"

POP
CORN

Then Mr. Muggs would

start the fire and

pop the corn.

They had a lot of fun together.

Ralph wished that they

could be together all the time.

He did not like it when

Mr. and Mrs. Muggs

went to work.

He sat on his perch

and sulked.

Then one day Mr. Mugg

the window open by mist

RALPH

At first Ralph

did not notice it.

He was sulking as usual.

Then he felt a breeze.

He saw that

the window was open.

It gave him

a wonderful idea.

He would fly out of the window!

He would fly down to the street!

He would make someone notice him

Ralph took off.

He did not

fly very well

because

he was not

used to flying.

When he reached the sidewal[k]

he almost landed on his tail.

He shook himself to be sure

nothing was broken.

Then he looked around.

Across the sidewalk

was a funny-looking red thing.

Ralph thought it would make

a good perch. He ran over to it.

He flew to the top

and rolled his eyes.

The street was crowded with people.

"Now I will whistle," thought Ralph.

"And someone will notice me."

Just then an old lady walked by.

Ralph whistled loudly.

The lady did not see Ralph.

She turned around and saw

a man walking behind her.

"Don't whistle at me, young man!"

she said.

The man looked surprised.

People laughed,

but no one noticed Ralph.

A mother and her little boy

came by.

Ralph tried again.

This time he said,

"Give me a cracker."

The mother did not see Ralph.

She said, "Billy, you just had

lunch."

The little boy looked surprised.

People heard her,

but no one noticed Ralph.

Then a boy and a girl went by.

They were having an argument.

The boy walked ahead.

He was mad.

Ralph said, "I love you!"

He hoped someone would

scratch him on the neck.

The boy turned around
and kissed the girl.
"I thought you were
mad at me," she said.

They held hands,
but no one noticed Ralph.

Ralph felt sad and cold.

He wanted to be inside

with Mr. and Mrs. Muggs

where it was warm and cozy.

Just then Ralph saw
something bright in
a window nearby.
It looked like the flames
in the fireplace at home.
"Fire," he said sadly.

"Fire," he said a little louder.

A tear rolled down his beak.

"Fire!" Ralph screamed.

A man in a big hat

heard him.

He stopped and

looked around.

He saw flames coming

from the window.

The man ran to

a phone booth.

In a few minutes

Ralph heard a loud siren.

A red fire truck raced up

to his perch and stopped.

A man in a rubber coat

ran over.

"At last someone has noticed me!"

Ralph thought.

But the fireman just picked him up

and put him in a tree.

People were shouting.

Smoke and water were

everywhere.

Ralph was frightened.

At last the fire was put out.

The man with the big hat

yelled, "Quiet!"

Everyone turned to look.

"This bird is a hero!" the man said.

Some of the people laughed.

They thought the man was joking.

"He was the one who yelled FIRE,"
the man said. "I noticed him when
I looked for a phone booth."

"Fire!" Ralph said happily.

Someone had noticed him!

"Oh!" said the people.

Then they cheered.

"What a smart bird,"

said a woman.

"He has saved lives,"

said the fireman.

"He should get a reward,"

said the man

in the big hat.

Just then Ralph saw

Mr. and Mrs. Muggs

coming home from work

"Hello, hello," he said.

Mr. and Mrs. Muggs

ran over to him.

"How did you get out here?"

asked Mrs. Muggs.

"What happened?" asked Mr. Muggs.

HELLO!

HELLO!

HELLO!

The man in the big hat

told them the story

of how Ralph had become a hero.

Mr. and Mrs. Muggs

were proud of him.

They scratched and tickled him.

Ralph got several rewards.

He got a ride in the fire truck.

He got his picture

in the newspaper.

He got free sesame-seed

crackers for life.

But best of all,

people noticed Ralph.

BONNIE BISHOP is a writer and artist who worked as an art director for a New York City publisher until several years ago when she and her husband moved to Cornville, Maine. There they built their own house in the woods and are enjoying life in the country.

JACK KENT is the author and illustrator of numerous funny books for children as well as the creator of the cartoon strip "King Aroo." Born in Burlington, Iowa, he has lived all over the United States, and now lives with his wife, June, in San Antonio, Texas.